STRAT.A.GEM

STRAT.A.GEM

RICK E. CUTTS

Library of Congress Control Number:		2021916315
ISBN:	Hardcover	978-1-6641-8956-0
	Softcover	978-1-6641-8955-3
	eBook	978-1-6641-8954-6

To order additional copies of this book, contact:
Xlibris
844-714-8691
www.Xlibris.com
Orders@Xlibris.com
833434

Acknowledgments

Writing a book is not anything I ever thought I could do. It is positively a task; however, it is very rewarding once you see the finished product. I would like to thank my mom and dad, Barbara and Ricky, as well as my older sister, Cynthia; her husband, Derrick; and my nephew, Simeon. Also, I would like to thank my children, Breanna and David, for providing me with all the motivation that I need to create a legacy for them for years to come. I positively have to thank my life partner, girlfriend, and best friend, Sully, for all the support and encouragement along the way.

I want to thank God for touching my mind and allowing me to utilize the gifts and talents I've been blessed with to hopefully help and inspire others.

Finally, a very special thanks to Ms. Reyna and the publishing team for the positive feedback and guidance along the way. There is no way that I could have gotten through this process without her and the team.

Enjoy!

Introduction

Rellik and his girlfriend, Nosaer, decide to accept an invitation to a party. Little do they know that life as they know it will change forever.

Follow Rellik and Nosaer on an amazing journey that takes them through twists and turns, all the while being chased by a mysterious killer. Can they escape? Will they escape? Who can they trust?

Follow them as you find out who is behind all the chaos suddenly upon Rellik and Nosaer as they discover how strong the bond between them really is—or will it be broken?

Rellik is about to leave a party with his girlfriend, Nosaer. Rellik and Nosaer witness a murder of a man as the killer dumps the body out of a truck. Rellik and Nosaer jump into a guy's car and ask his name. The guy says that his name is Enoon. They tell Enoon that they just saw someone get killed and need to escape. Enoon agrees and tries to drive away without being noticed.

The guy from the truck starts following them.

Rellik instructs Enoon where to drive to try to escape the driver in the truck. The trio—Rellik, Nosaer, and Enoon— smoothly escapes and arrives at a house where Rellik knows a couple of the people. Rellik approaches Demetri and asks if it is

OK for the trio to lie low there for a little while.

It is a small gathering of people socializing, and Demetri tells Rellik of course he can stay. Rellik and Nosaer sit off by themselves in a corner room. He tells Nosaer about the dream of them catching a flight and being together. There is music playing, and they decide to tell those at the party what they witnessed earlier.

Rellik tells them about witnessing a murder and running away. The patrons in the house kind of think it is a joke and say Rellik should go to the police, joking and laughing about it. Someone turns the music back up, and soon everyone is back to partying.

Eventually, everyone falls asleep or passes out.

Rellik wakes suddenly from a bad dream as he and Nosaer rest on the couch. Rellik hears a knock at the door. The others in the house seem to be asleep, and Nosaer tells Rellik to see who could be at the door. Rellik walks toward the door and notices Enoon opening it. It is hard for Rellik to see who is at the door, but then he realizes it is the guy they witnessed killing someone the previous night.

Rellik quickly closes the door, locks it, grabs Nosacr, and says, "We've got to get outta here."

The killer throws some type of gas into the house through the windows. Rellik runs to try to wake up the others who are sleeping and realizes that those still in the house are not sleeping.

They are all dead.

Except Demetri. Demetri is holding on to just a little bit of life. He asks Rellik, "Why did this happen?" as he passes away.

Rellik grabs Nosaer and notices as they escape out the back door that Nosaer inhaled some of the toxic gas and has a cut from the shrapnel hitting her. She can't breathe and keeps saying she is thirsty. The cut starts changing colors.

Rellik and Nosaer are running in between houses while trying to get away. He does not see Enoon and does not know if he made it out of the house safely. While running, they stumble onto some kids having a tea party.

Quickly, Rellik asks if he can have something to drink for his lady, Nosaer. Instantly, the kids give them a cup of tea. There is nothing in the cup! It is a make-believe tea party.

Rellik takes Nosaer and continues to run to try to find help for her.

They finally come upon a house where a lady comes to the door.

Rellik is holding Nosaer and asks the lady to please give him some water for Nosaer, and he asks the lady to call an ambulance. The lady asks him for his name, and Rellik lets her know that his name is Rellik Nalp. The lady tells him that her name is Kira Petrov and invites him in.

As Rellik is about to turn the corner, he sees one of the people whom he saw earlier that night and gets a funny feeling that the guy could be with the killer he has been running from. Rellik backs up before the guy at the table sees him and runs out the door with Nosaer. Rellik sees a car with guns and bombs in it—the same stuff he saw when he was at Demetri's house before everyone got killed.

Rellik and Nosaer calmly get into the car and notices that the place they are at is full of bad guys. Just as they are about to leave, Kira goes to the door and speaks in Russian to the guys just as another car of henchmen pulls up. They see Rellik, and one screams, "Not again! Where is he going? Catch him!"

Police sirens are going off now as well. Someone called about the fire and shots they heard at Demetri's place.

Just as Rellik and Nosaer are trying to calmly pass the police, they are summoned by the police to stop. Rellik is very nervous because the car is full of guns and explosives. Just then, another explosion goes off, and a police officer waves Rellik to keep driving as officers go toward the explosion, allowing Rellik and Nosaer to escape.

A flashback shows that Rellik planted the explosive to go off in the house with Kira and the bad guys. Now excited, Rellik tells Nosaer that they escaped and that they can go to the airport and go away to be together. Rellik looks over and realizes that Nosaer is unresponsive and her skin is looking bad. The poison is taking over her body, and Rellik begins to cry.

Just before Rellik completely breaks down, Nosaer regains consciousness. She tells Rellik in a weak voice, "I know that I truly love you. I know it."

Rellik asks, "How do you know? Because I really love you too."

Nosaer then says again in a weak voice, "I know that I love you. I was hesitant at first, but now I really know." Rellik looks puzzled and says, "How?"

Nosaer says, "When you killed all those people at the party at Demetri's house, I was thinking about leaving, also when you threw the guy out of the car, but then I thought maybe I should stay with him because he seems like he's still a good person."

Nosaer lets Rellik know that she is not scared to die and then asks him not to kill himself along with everyone on the plane.

Rellik looks at Nosaer, confused, and says he's not going to kill people on a plane or himself. Rellik also says that he didn't kill anyone but the bad guys from Kira's house they just left.

A flashback shows Rellik on a mission to take down the Mafia and blow up a plane with the group of Russian Mafia guys who killed his family when he was a young boy. He knew that they were going on a certain plane with drugs and money.

Another flashback shows that in the beginning, the person who threw the dead body out of the car was Rellik. The first killing was one of the Mafia guys who killed Rellik's family when he was a boy. The car that Rellik jumped into was a car that he stole. There was no other guy in the car. Enoon doesn't exist! Enoon is just "no one" spelled backward! That is just in his mind.

The house where Demetri was that Rellik and Nosaer drove was a part of the same Russian Mafia. He pretended that he was trying to escape and that people were after him. It was Rellik who killed everyone at

Demetri's house. One of the guys from the Mafia saw Rellik when he killed the first guy and threw him out of the car and went to Demetri's house that morning to warn Demitri when Rellik spotted him.

Enoon was never at the door to see who it was. It was Rellik who went to the door and noticed that the guy at the door was one of the Mafia guys who spotted him, so Rellik gassed and shot up the house and killed those in the house before running to get away.

Rellik accidentally hit his girlfriend, Nosaer, with the poison.

When Rellik escaped with Nosaer and went to Kira Petrov's house, he knew that she was the leader of the Mafia, Victor Petrov's wife, and a partner in the business. Rellik was not counting on the one guy who got away being at Kira's house, so Rellik had to blow up the house and kill everyone in it so that he and Nosaer could get away.

Rellik was on the way to the airport with the explosives to kill the rest of the Russian Mafia. Rellik's plan was to kill all of the Mafia with the same explosives and poison gas that was used to kill his family. Rellik's plan was to commit suicide and allow Nosaer to live in peace without any fear of being chased.

Rellik knew that after he infiltrated the gang and got to be close with Demitri as well as most of the other Mafia bosses, he would be hunted forever. Rellik figured as long as he took out those who killed his family, he could die in peace.

Nosaer didn't want Rellik to kill himself. (That was what they were discussing when they were at Demetri's house.)

A flashback shows Rellik telling Nosaer to take his life savings and start a new life. Nosaer was trying to let Rellik know that they could run away together, but he refused and then proceeded to carry out his plan.

Now everything goes back to the present with Nosaer sharing a final kiss with Rellik. After the kiss, Nosaer passes away. Rellik realizes that he was the mastermind of everything. He realizes that Enoon was an alter ego he created to assist him mentally with carrying out his plan, and Nosaer was really the only reason he was motivated to live. Now that she's gone, he just feels lost.

A scene flashes back to when Rellik and Nosaer first met. Rellik was in the process of doing recon on the Russian Mafia. He was attractive, tall, dressed very nice, and smelled amazing. Nosaer was a lively, athletic woman with beautiful, long hair working as a nurse whose bosses' facility got destroyed by the Russian Mafia for not giving them a cut of the business.

Rellik met Nosaer as she was outside in tears over the business being destroyed and her boss being killed while she was out of the office. Rellik asked her name, and she said Rosalinda. They formed a bond, friendship, and relationship as he assisted her getting back on her feet.

Rellik gave Rosalinda the nickname Nosaer after Rellik reminisced on when they met. The scene flashes back to him in the car with Nosaer passing away. Rellik continues to the airport where the Mafia is and blows up the plane, killing everyone.

A flashback shows Rellik's family being killed by the Russian Mafia for not selling the business. That is why he bonded with

Nosaer. It made him think of what happened to him as a child, and he wanted to help her.

Rellik was just a young boy at the time, playing in the underpart of the business where he would often hide and play. The Mafia was laughing and throwing the different gases into the business and brutally slaying his parents, his older brother, and both sisters before setting everything on fire.

Rellik crawled out of the space out the back and walked the streets. Rellik would often take apples from an apple tree that he found and steal whatever food he could find. One day he was caught taking apples from the fruit tree to eat. The man who caught him was an old war vet that everyone called Doc.

Doc asked the young man what his name was, and the young man didn't speak. Doc told him that he would have to work to eat the apples and any other food. Doc told the young man that he didn't have to steal ever and that he needed to earn everything he ate. There was a rage, fearlessness, and anger that Doc saw in him.

Doc saw that the boy was homeless with tattered clothes and needed guidance. He took the boy in, trained him, and raised him as his own. Doc learned what happened to the boy's parents and worked to give him focus, hope, and purpose. Doc started calling the boy John. One day John told him that his name died with his family and that he set forth a plan to kill those responsible for his family's death.

His new name would be Rellik Nalp, which in reverse spelt "Killer Plan."

Doc knew that if he didn't help him, no matter what, Rellik would go after those who killed his family. Doc began training him brutally. He trained him in weapons, bomb-making, hand-to-hand combat, and military attack formations. He also showed him how to dress, blend in with anyone, and become anyone he needed to be.

Rellik was determined and learned everything necessary to prepare him for his suicide mission.

Fast-forward to the present time and Rellik walks from the flames with Nosaer. He places a bandage on her wound and dresses it. Rellik places a needle into her heart with an antidote to try to combat the gas she accidentally got hit with.

Nosaer slowly opens her eyes and is still alive. Rellik says, "Now I have a reason to live again. My Nosaer is back."

Nosaer is "reason" spelled backward. Rellik nicknamed her that because she was his reason.

A flashback shows that Rellik saw a first aid kit with the things necessary for him to administer the antidote to Nosaer. He grabbed it and Nosaer. Rellik exited the car before he sent it into the plane with the explosives, with both of them getting safely out.

Nosaer smiles as the ambulance arrives.

Rellik watches from the side as she gets into the ambulance, and he mouths the words "I love you" to her.

At the hospital, Rellik shows up in Nosaer's room dressed as the doctor and takes Nosaer out of the hospital. Doc waits on them in a car.

Once in the car, Doc looks at Rellik and says, "Man, that really was a killer plan."

They laugh and then Doc asks him, "By the way, what is your real name anyway? I can't walk around calling you Rellik Nalp all the time."

Rellik looks at Doc and Nosaer and says, "My real name is Adrian Golden."

Doc and Nosaer look at one another. They pause for a few moments and then Doc says,

"You know what I think? We will call you Rellik. It fits you better."

They all laugh.

Rellik asks Doc, "What's your real name?"

Doc says, "Ummm. That's classified." He winks at them both and drives off.

As they drive off, Doc says, "I'll tell you one thing. My name is better than Adrian Golden."

About the Author

Rick E. Cutts was born in 1978 in Chicago, Illinois. He grew up in a creative household, and his parents always encouraged him to read and often presented puzzles or thought-provoking questions to make him think. That is where his passion for mysteries and trying to guess how a story ends started.

Most of the time, he guesses the endings and wishes for more unpredictable endings.

That same passion is what led Rick to write his own stories with plenty of twists and turns that have readers guessing all the way through!

In *Stratagem,* he takes readers through a young man's journey full of exciting thrills. It's a ride like never before! Get ready to dig in to see what happens as you will be on the edge of your seat until the very end. With an unpredictable ending.